CAZAQ THE EAGLE

TERESA SKINNER

CAZAQ THE EAGLE

Coloring Book

ISBN: 978-1-950123-87-2

Originally published as "Casaq the Eagle" hardcover 2009 Teresa Skinner

Written by Teresa Skinner

Illustrated by Julian P. V. Arias and Patrick Joe Pulliam

Editor: Marsha Bonfluer

Consultants: Marilyn Bread, Kiowa Nation

Norma Blacksmith, Lakota Nation

Information on the American Bald Eagle © 2009 by American Eagle Foundation Used by permission www.eagles.org

Want to read more books like this?

Visit https://teresaskinner.com

CAZAQ THE EAGLE

Listen, my children as I tell you a story about an Eagle. Once upon a time in the land where the flute sings with the wind and the drum beats to the heartbeat of life, there lived two Eagles… Two Eagles returned to the Mountain of Hope to make a nest. Soon Father and Mother Eagle took turns sitting quietly on their three eggs, keeping them warm from the harsh weather and cool from the hot sun.

Suddenly...

...a great thunderstorm came with a great wind and terrible darkness.

The storm blew right through the nest, surprising Father and Mother Eagle. Though the Eagles had braced themselves and their nest from the storm, somehow one Lonely Egg fell from the nest.

Merciful Creator watched as Lonely Egg fell… so far. He allowed a tree with its soft leaves to break Lonely Egg's fall. For a moment Lonely Egg was safe.

After the storm left, Lonely Egg could not be found… Father and Mother Eagle searched but he was nowhere to be found. Then one last wind came, and Lonely Egg fell again, only to roll onto the soft grass and land next to a rock.

Young Shepherd, son of Father Farmer was tending his Sheep like he did every day. The thunderstorm had stopped. Young Shepherd counted his Sheep, concerned that he may have lost some baby lambs in the storm. They were all safe. Young Shepherd learned well from his Uncle, how to keep the flock together and safe during a storm.

Young Shepherd would return in the morning early. For now he hurried home knowing that a warm meal was waiting, prepared for him by his mother. As Young Shepherd ran past the fearful Mountain of Hope, he looked up. It was such a tall Mountain that the clouds would cover the top.

Oops, Young Shepherd tripped over a rock. What was this?

Young Shepherd picked up Lonely Egg and carried it home in his hand trying to keep it warm.

Young Shepherd went to the chicken yard and found the Biggest Chicken.

Please, Mother Chicken, you have room for one more. Take this egg and raise it; you know what to do.

Mother Chicken squawked as Young Shepherd quickly put Lonely Egg under her. Lonely Egg was very big compared to the other eggs she had hatched. But Mother Chicken loved Young Shepherd and sat on Lonely Egg for a long time.

All of Mother Chicken's eggs had hatched. Baby chicks ran everywhere.

Six days later, Lonely Egg still had not hatched. Finally, on the seventh day, Lonely Egg violently shook and rocked back and forth. Mother Chicken was startled!

A large beak broke through the shell, then, a gray furry head popped out! "This is not the same color as my other baby chicks; it is so strong and big," said Mother Chicken. Lonely Egg rocked back and forth until finally all of the shell was off and a baby eaglet lay on the ground.

"Come and play with us…"

"…come and play! We can eat grain and chase the other baby chicks," said Brother and Sister Chicken.

Mother Chicken quickly replied, "Leave him alone; he will come when he is ready."

Lonely Egg lay in the nest and Mother Chicken kept him warm. Merciful Creator told Mother Chicken to give Lonely Egg worms and not grain like the other chicks. Lonely Egg could not run and play with the other baby chicks. He was so big and clumsy that when Brother and Sister Chicken would run fast, he would trip over his big talons. As Lonely Egg grew, the other chickens noticed his size and laughed at him.

One stern look from Mother Chicken's eye would silence all of them. Soon, all of the barn animals accepted Lonely Egg, even though he was so large and did not eat grain like the other chickens.

Weeks passed by and Lonely Egg grew larger and stronger than his Brothers and Sisters. Ravens and other animals were afraid of him and would not come around to steal the chickens. The chickens named Lonely Egg, "Cazaq" or Hope because as long as he was there they knew they would be safe.

Merciful Creator allowed the story of the large eagle that lived with the chickens to come to Mountain Range of Hope, where many eagles fly.

Three eagles, Wisda, Deter and Compa were elected by the Eagle Clan to fly to Father Farmer's chicken yard to see this large bird.

When they arrived, they were shocked. "How can this be? An Eagle with his head down and scratching for food like a chicken," said Wisda. "How did this Eagle get here?" asked Deter. "Could this be the egg that dropped from Mountain of Hope many years ago?" wondered Compa.

Wisda, Deter and Compa watched from a distance. They shook their heads in disbelief to see Merciful Creator's powerful Eagle, Cazaq, who did not know who he was, looking down to the ground scratching for worms just like a chicken.

Wisda, Deter and Compa needed to devise a plan to help Cazaq realize who he was – a powerful Eagle. Wisda and Compa flew very high to the highest winds and consulted with Merciful Creator as Deter flew around the chicken yard and watched Cazaq closely.

Deter's shadow fell across Cazaq and all of the chickens in the yard. The chickens ran for cover, they were afraid a raven was coming to take one of them away.

Cazaq was fighting with a worm and did not notice the shadow because his head was always down.

Deter dropped to the ground next to Cazaq.

Deter spoke to Cazaq, but Cazaq was afraid and ran behind Mother Chicken. Mother Chicken trembled with fear too when she saw Deter but determined she would give her life to protect Cazaq.

Deter said with a strong and powerful voice, "Mother Chicken, tell Cazaq who he is. I will return soon and teach him to fly." Then the shadow left.

Mother Chicken told Cazaq the story as she had heard it from Young Shepherd when he told Father Farmer. She told him he was found at the bottom of Mountain of Hope and that the next time Deter came for him he must not be afraid but go with him. Mother Chicken told Cazaq he was not a chicken but an Eagle. Cazaq was sad and afraid, but all of the chickens cooed Cazaq, encouraging him to go with Deter.

They asked Cazaq not to forget them

Sometime later the shadow came again, the chickens ran for cover. Again, Cazaq had his head down and did not notice the shadow.

Wisda, Deter and Compa flew over Cazaq and all at once, without warning, dove for Cazaq. Together they lifted this great bird into the sky.

The three Eagles carried Cazaq up, up toward the clouds. He was so afraid. Then, when they were high enough, they let Cazaq go.

Cazaq fell.

He seemed to remember this feeling; he did not like it. Cazaq was terrified!

The three Eagles flew next to Cazaq. "Open your wings" Deter instructed. "Do not be afraid," shouted Compa. "You are an Eagle!" cried Wisda.

Right before Cazaq hit the ground; the three Eagles caught him with their strong wings and carried him even higher.

Wisda said, "Watch us and do what we do."

Again, they dropped Cazaq.

For the first time in his life, Cazaq lifted his head and saw the other eagles fly.

Cazaq stretched out his wings and flapped them, "I am flying!"

He broke his own fall and landed safely but roughly.

Wisda, Deter and Compa landed next to him. "From now on hold your head up, look around you and learn," encouraged Deter. "Flap your wings everyday so that you may become strong and out fly the strongest storm," explained Compa. "We will return," said Wisda.

When Cazaq returned to the chicken yard he was very excited. "I am an Eagle!" Cazaq said proudly. Soon Cazaq became arrogant with Mother Chicken and the other farm animals.

One day, as Cazaq boasted about who he was, all the animals ignored him and a large shadow swooped down and took Sister Chicken.

All of the chickens squawked in horror, "Return Sister Chicken, you evil Mr. Raven, return Sister Chicken!" Cazaq had not noticed the shadow because in his arrogance all he could notice was himself. When Cazaq heard the cry of the chickens he shook himself and flew after Mr. Raven startling Mr. Raven and making him drop Sister Chicken.

After placing Sister Chicken on the ground safely, Cazaq apologized for his arrogance. He had forgotten to keep his head up AND look around and learn. Had he kept his focus Mr. Raven would not have been able to take Sister Chicken.

Cazaq carefully watched the chicken yard daily.

Some time had passed...

...and Cazaq heard a screech that was familiar to him. Cazaq looked up and saw Deter calling to him. Cazaq flew to Deter and together the powerful Eagles flew very high. Deter taught Cazaq how to fly through the storm. He taught Cazaq how to hunt and how to fight.

After several days Deter left, and Wisda taught Cazaq when and how to fly above the storm. He taught Cazaq about Merciful Creator and the dangers of arrogance and pride. Wisda showed Cazaq the Mountain Range of Hope. Wisda then took Cazaq to the highest mountain and told him to rest and feed. They would return soon.

The time had come when his friends would leave him. He thanked them for their patience and kindness. He promised them he would return to the Mountain Range of Hope to live one day.

Cazaq flew to Father Farmer's chicken yard. He thanked Brother and Sister Chicken. He flew to Young Shepherd's flock and thanked Young Shepherd for his kindness. Cazaq warned the Ravens to find other places to eat. By doing this he showed gratitude to Old Father Farmer.

He told Mother Chicken that he would fly far away and he would not return this time. Mother Chicken wiped away a tear and blessed Cazaq with this blessing:

"When the Eagle lifts up his head and realizes who Merciful Creator has made him to be, and when the Eagle is willing to forgive Mother Storm, Sister Wind and Brother Circumstance who brought him low, then Merciful Creator will smile on the Eagle and restore his strength and will give him the power of His Spirit. He will use the Eagle to bring His pleasure to the earth. Then and only then will you be able to 'Mount up With Wings as Eagles'. "

Cazaq flapped his wings and flying high in the sky, he sang a new song with all of his heart, "I forgive you!" he sang to the wind, "I am free now!" he sang to himself, "I can fly to the heartbeat of life!

Cazaq go, and do not forget where you came from.

Now you will fly with Wisdom,

Determination,

Compassion,

and Mercy.

Yes Cazaq, it is your time.